SNOWBOUND

ARTHUR ROTH

Photographs by Paul DeGeorges

Copyright © 1989, 1975 by Arthur Roth.
All rights reserved. Published by Scholastic Inc.
SPRINT and SPRINT BOOKS are trademarks of Scholastic Inc.
Printed in the U.S.A.
ISBN 0-590-35195-8

8 9 10   31   03 02 01 00 99

CHAPTER 1

"I think we're in for a blizzard!" Mr. Mitchell said into the kitchen phone. He was talking to his wife.

Pat looked up at her father. They had just finished dinner when the call came. Pat and her parents lived on Deer Island. Right now, Mrs. Mitchell was away on the mainland, visiting her father.

"Heavy snow warnings," Mr. Mitchell said to his wife. "They're talking about 60-mile-an-hour winds. You'd better stay where you are, at least for another day. Besides, the ferry isn't going to run in this weather." He handed the phone to Pat. "Here, Pat. Your mother wants to talk to you."

Pat took the phone. "Hi, Mom," she said. "How are you?"

"I'm fine, honey. But I'm worried about Mrs. Lester. Her husband is away fishing. And her baby has the flu. With a snowstorm coming, she may need some help. Call her later tonight and see if there's anything you can do."

"Sure, Mom."

"Good girl. Bye-bye now. Take good care of yourself."

"OK, Mom." Pat hung up. Then she sat down at the table again. Her father poured himself a cup of coffee. Pat went back to the subject they had been talking about at dinner.

"A trail bike is very safe, Dad, honestly." Pat had been saving her money for a long time. Now she had almost enough to buy a trail bike. But she had to persuade her father to let her get one.

"You start taking better care of your things," her father said. "Then we'll talk about a trail bike."

"Aw, Dad, I take care of my things."

"What about the 10-speed bike you got last summer?" her father asked. "You left it out in the rain and the snow. Now it's covered with rust."

Pat had no answer for that. She had lost interest in her 10-speed after she took a ride on a friend's trail bike.

"And how about your grades?" her father asked. "You're almost failing math. And you're not doing too well in history, either."

"I'll pass, Dad, honest," Pat said.

"I'll tell you what," said her father. "Let's see how you do in the next two months. Try to pull up your grades. And be more careful about looking after your things. Then we'll have another talk about the trail bike."

Pat didn't like what her father was saying. Two months seemed like forever. Maybe she could get her father to change his mind. But now wasn't the right time to try. She decided to change the subject.

"Say, Dad, March 30 is pretty late for a

blizzard, isn't it?"

"Yes, it's a bit late. Still, I remember one bad storm as late as April," her father said. "It was the year your mother and I got married. We had 16 inches of snow on the fourth of April. Talk about a surprise! On the mainland, it blocked every road for miles."

"Wow, 16 inches!" Pat said.

"That's right," said her father. He got up from the table and went to the phone. "I'd better call the men."

Pat's father had a small business of his own. He built driveways, sank wells, and dug out cellars. He looked after the island's three or four main roads. Part of his job was to keep the roads free of snow. He also had to clear snow from the streets of Homeport. Homeport was Deer Island's only village.

Most of the island men were fishermen. The fishing fleet had left the day before. The boats were headed for the cod fishing banks off Newfoundland. With the fleet gone, there were only a few men left on the island to help out during the snowstorm. Three of those men worked for Pat's father.

"Hello, Bill," Pat's father said over the phone. "Now they're saying 10 inches. Just go back and forth on 67. Try to keep French Cut open. Right."

Mr. Mitchell hung up. Then he dialed another number. "Right, Wesley," Mr. Mitchell said. "Start

with the fishing dock. Then do the fire station. We'll be in touch. 'Bye."

Mr. Mitchell had four trucks with snowplows. But one of the trucks was out of action. The gas tank on the outside of the truck had broken off a month ago. A falling boulder had knocked it loose. A new tank had been ordered. But it hadn't arrived yet.

Mr. Mitchell picked up the phone again. He dialed the number of his foreman, Rod

Anderson. Mrs. Anderson answered the phone. "What?" asked Mr. Mitchell. "Rod went to the mainland this morning? He was supposed to be back by now? Well, he won't make it. There's no way the ferry will run tonight. Don't worry, we're fine. Yes. Good-bye." Mr. Mitchell hung up the phone.

"What is it, Dad?" Pat asked.

"Rod had to go to the mainland this morning. He's not back yet. I'll have to take out the radio truck myself."

Only one of Mr. Mitchell's trucks had a citizens' band radio. The other radio unit was in the Mitchell kitchen. During a snowstorm, Mr. Mitchell ran his crew from the house. Now he looked over at his daughter. "I'll need your help, Pat," he said. "You'll have to work the radio here."

"Me? Wow! Sure, Dad." Pat went over and sat down in front of the radio.

"All right, calm down," Mr. Mitchell said. "I won't be leaving for another half hour." He paused for a moment and looked at his daughter closely. "This is a big responsibility, Pat. Are you sure you can handle it?"

"Don't worry, Dad," Pat replied. "You can count on me."

"I hope so," said Mr. Mitchell. He smiled at Pat. Then he began to get ready for the long night ahead.

CHAPTER 2

Pat could hardly sit still. She would be running the whole crew by herself! She would be telling everyone what to do and where to go.

Wow, would Judy O'Connor and Vicky Dawson be jealous! They were Pat's best friends. They lived just down the road.

Pat went over to the back door and looked out. The snow was coming down in blinding white sheets.

"Hey, it's really getting heavy, Dad!"

"I know," replied her father. "It's going to be a bad storm."

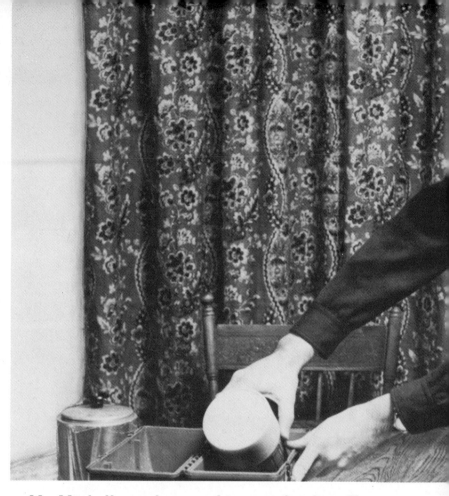

Mr. Mitchell was busy making sandwiches. He didn't know how long he would be gone. He had often worked all night during a storm.

"I'll get the thermos, Dad," said Pat. She rinsed out the thermos with hot water. Then she poured coffee into it.

"I want you to listen in on the police band," Mr. Mitchell said. "You can keep me up to date on what is going on."

"Sure, Dad. How much sugar?"

"Two spoons. And if you can't get hold of me, don't panic. I might be outside of the truck. I

might not hear your call. Or I could be helping Wes or Bill."

"OK, Dad. I'll just keep calling."

Mr. Mitchell put the sandwiches and thermos in his lunch box. Then he got into his heavy jacket. He zipped up the hood.

"Here is your flashlight, Dad," said Pat.

Mr. Mitchell took the flashlight. "OK, you know how to work all the equipment. I'm going straight into Homeport. Good-bye, honey. And good luck."

Pat said good-bye to her father. Then she sat

down in front of the CB radio. Beside it was an FM/AM radio with weather and police bands.

A few minutes later the CB began to squawk. "KLI 21-21, calling KLI 21-21. Unit One to Base. How is everything?"

Pat picked up the mike. She pushed the button and said, "Hi, Dad, this is me, Pat."

"Give me your call numbers," her father said.

"Oh, sure," Pat said. "This is KLI 21-21. Base to Unit One. Go ahead, Unit One."

"KLI 21-21, Unit One to Base. Everything is fine here. Just running an equipment check. Signing off now. Over."

"Base to Unit One," Pat said. "Everything is fine here. Good luck, Dad. Over."

Pat set the mike down. Then the phone rang. She jumped up to get the call.

"Joe, this is Mrs. Quigley. I've run out of oil. The oil truck can't make it up my driveway. Henry says you have to come plow me out."

"This is Pat Mitchell, Mrs. Quigley. My dad is out on one of the plows. I'll call and tell him."

"Oh, would you, like a good girl? Thank you very much. And please tell your father to hurry. It's starting to get cold."

"All right, Mrs. Quigley. I'll tell him."

Pat reached her dad on the CB. She gave him Mrs. Quigley's message.

"OK, Pat. I'll have Wesley plow out her driveway. Call her back and tell her that a plow will be there in ten minutes. Then call Island Fuel. Tell Henry that Mrs. Quigley's driveway is being plowed."

"Right, Dad."

Pat made the two calls. Two minutes after she hung up, the phone rang again. This time it was Doc Miller. "Someone is bringing in a sick baby," the doctor said. "I have to get plowed out."

"I'll call my dad and tell him," Pat said.

"Tell him he has to come right away. This is urgent," Doc Miller warned.

"Yes, sir!"

Pat managed to get hold of her father. She told him what Doctor Miller wanted.

"Well, I have Bill plowing French Cut," said Mr. Mitchell. "And Wesley is at Mrs. Quigley's. That leaves me. You call Doc Miller back. Tell him I'm on the way. And call Mrs. Quigley."

"I already called her, Dad," Pat said.

"Call her again. Tell her to have Wesley call you when he is through there. Tell Wesley to head for the police station in Homeport. I'll call him there."

"OK. So long for now, Dad."

Pat made the phone calls to Doctor Miller and Mrs. Quigley. Then she went over to the back door and put on the outside light. The snow had been piling up for a while. Pat wondered how deep it was. She took a 12-inch ruler outside and stuck it in the snow. The snow came up to the six-inch mark.

Pat whistled. Six inches already! She left the ruler in the snow so she could look out the back door and see it.

CHAPTER 3

The phone was ringing when Pat got back inside. "Hello?" she said breathlessly.

"This is Peggy Lester. My little Matthew is very sick. I have to take him to Doctor Miller's."

"Mrs. Lester, this is Pat. My father is in Homeport. He's on one of the snowplows."

"What am I going to do? My car is stuck in the driveway. The baby has a temperature of 106. I'm afraid he will go into convulsions. I just have to get him over to Doc Miller's clinic."

"I can get my dad on the radio, Mrs. Lester. He's probably at Doctor Miller's place right now. He could reach you in half an hour."

"Please call him and tell him. I'm so frightened. Please get hold of your daddy."

"Right away," Pat promised. She hung up the phone and went over to the radio. "KLI 21-21, calling KLI 21-21. Base to Unit One. Come in, Dad."

Silence. Pat called again. Still no answer. She waited a minute or two. Then she tried a third time. Again, no answer. Now what should she do? Her father could be outside the truck fixing the blade on the plow. Or maybe his radio was broken.

Pat felt bad. She had promised her mother that she would call Mrs. Lester. But in all the excitement, she had forgotten to make the call. Now Mrs. Lester might not be able to get the

help she needed. And Pat was sure that it was all her fault.

She went to the phone and called Doctor Miller. He said that Pat's father hadn't arrived. Pat went back to the radio and tried to call her dad. For over ten minutes she kept trying. But she had no luck.

Pat went back to the phone and called Mrs. Lester. She explained that she couldn't reach her father.

"The baby will surely die if I don't get him to a doctor," Mrs. Lester said.

"Maybe I could dig out your car," said Pat.

"Would you, Pat? Just to give me a good start down the driveway. I can make it after that. I'm sure the plows are keeping the road open."

"I'll be right over, Mrs. Lester," Pat said. She hung up the phone. Then she tried the radio once more. There was still no answer from her dad. Pat got into her boots and put on her heavy

jacket. Her dad had said not to leave the radio. But her mother had said to help Mrs. Lester in any way she could. Maybe it wouldn't take long to dig out the car. Then Pat could get home before her dad missed her.

She put on her gloves and picked up a flashlight. It wasn't far to Mrs. Lester's house. Pat could walk there in ten minutes. She opened the door and stepped outside. A blast of cold air hit her in the face.

Soon Pat was out on the open road. Here the snow had drifted into knee-deep piles. That was bad, she thought. The snow drifts would make it hard for Mrs. Lester to drive to Doc Miller's.

The wind drove into Pat like a football tackle. She had trouble catching her breath. Finally, she turned around and walked backward for a while.

After a while Pat turned back into the wind again. Bent double, she pushed ahead. Finally, she came to the Lesters' house. She walked up the driveway and looked at the car. The front wheels were hidden in a pile of snow. The back wheels were off the edge of the drive.

"Oh, Pat, thank goodness you came," cried Mrs. Lester. She was standing at the back door. She held out a shovel. "Here, I found this in the garage. Can you dig out the car?"

"I think so." Pat took the shovel.

Pat began to shovel the snow away from the

front of the car. Soon she had the front wheels
uncovered. Next she worked at the back of the
car. Snow flew every which way from her shovel.

Finally, the rear wheels were free.

Pat went to the back door and shouted into the kitchen. "Mrs. Lester? You're ready to go."

CHAPTER 4

Mrs. Lester came out of the house, carrying the baby in a small wicker basket. Pat opened the car door, and Mrs. Lester got inside with the baby.

"Do you want a ride, Pat?" Mrs. Lester asked.

"No," said Pat. Her house was in the opposite direction. "Once you start, don't stop for anything. I'll give you a push."

Pat turned her back to the trunk of the car. Then she bent her knees and gripped the bumper with her hands. Lifting and pushing at the same time, she shoved hard. Bits of snow

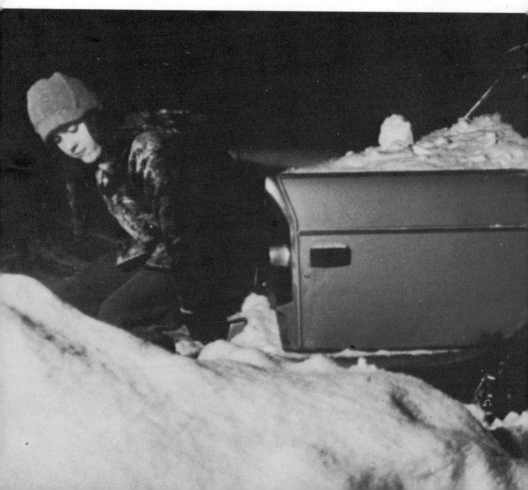

flew back from the spinning wheels. Pat felt the car move an inch. "Good," she grunted. She gave an extra heave. Suddenly the car took hold and shot forward. Pat lost her balance and nearly fell.

She watched the car move down the driveway. It looked as if Mrs. Lester would make it. The red taillights grew bright as she began to brake. She had to turn onto the road.

Suddenly the car went sideways. "Oh, no!" Pat cried out. She watched the car slide off the driveway. It skidded onto the snow-covered lawn and stalled.

Mrs. Lester got out of the car with the baby. Pat ran over to them. "We'll have to go back to the house," cried Mrs. Lester. "You go ahead with the flashlight. I'll carry the baby."

Shining the light, Pat broke a trail for Mrs. Lester. Soon they were back inside the kitchen. Mrs. Lester put the baby on top of the kitchen table. Every breath the baby took came with an awful rattle. Pat got a look at his face. It was a whitish-blue color. She wondered why he didn't cry. He probably needs all his strength just to breathe, she thought.

Pat wasn't sure what to do. She could hike home and try to get her father on the radio. Or maybe her friend Judy O'Connor could help. The O'Connors had a snowmobile. Then Pat thought of the police.

"I know, Mrs. Lester. We can call the police," Pat said. "The Chief will know how to get my father."

"Oh, yes. That's a good idea," Mrs. Lester said. "Will you call him, Pat? I want to rub the baby with a little alcohol. That will keep the fever down."

Pat dialed the police number. Chief Campbell picked up the phone. Pat told him about Mrs. Lester's sick baby.

"I don't know where your dad is, Pat," the Chief said. "But I can send Patrolman Russo in the jeep. It has snow tires and four-wheel drive.

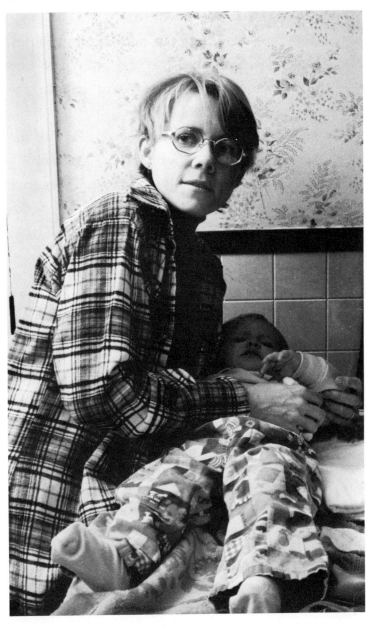

Can you stay with Mrs. Lester until Russo gets there?"

"Yes, sir."

"Good. I'll keep trying to reach your father.

I'll let him know where you are."

"Thank you." Pat hung up and turned around. Mrs. Lester was bending over the baby. She had a wad of cotton in her hand. Pat caught the smell of rubbing alcohol.

"Mrs. Lester, the Chief says help is on the way. Patrolman Russo is coming in his jeep."

Mrs. Lester looked up. For a moment her face lost its frightened look. "Thank goodness," she said. "That's marvelous. You were so smart to think of the police."

Pat felt a little guilty about being praised. She had told her mother she would call Mrs. Lester. But instead she had forgotten all about her.

"Would you care for a sandwich, Pat?" Mrs. Lester asked. "You must be hungry."

"No, thanks," Pat said.

"There is some ice cream in the freezer," Mrs. Lester said. "Let me get you some." She brought Pat a dish of chocolate ice cream. Then she went back to sponging the baby.

A little while later, Patrolman Russo arrived. "If you're ready, we should go right now," he told them. "When I came through French Cut, I talked to Bill. He said he couldn't keep the cut open much longer. The snow is getting too deep."

Mrs. Lester already had her coat on. She picked up the baby and followed Patrolman Russo out to the jeep. Mrs. Lester sat up front,

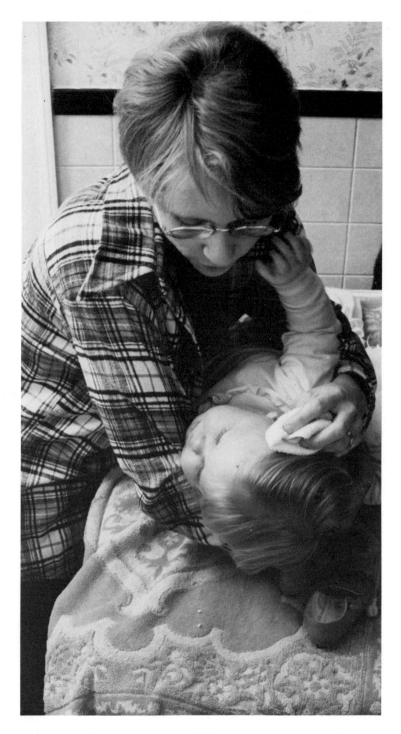

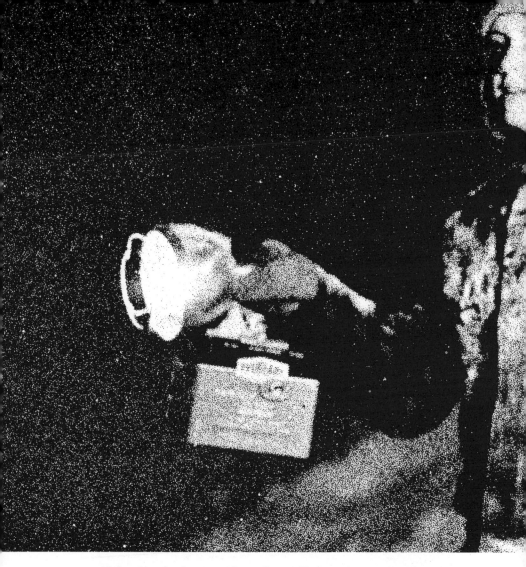

with the baby on her lap. Pat sat in the back.
There was a bad moment as they inched past
the stalled car. But then they turned onto the
road. Pat tapped Patrolman Russo on the arm. "I
can walk home from here," she said.

"Are you sure?" he asked. "I can run you
home. But I really should push on in case French
Cut closes up."

"You go ahead," Pat said. She showed the

policeman her flashlight. "I have a light here. Anyway, it's only a short walk."

Pat got out of the jeep and waved good-bye. Then she began pushing her way through the drifts. It was tough going. In one spot the snow was up to her waist. All the way home, Pat kept wondering about one thing. Would the jeep make it through French Cut and get the baby to Doc Miller in time?

CHAPTER 5

What should have been a ten-minute walk turned into a half-hour struggle through snowdrifts and over icy roads. Finally, Pat reached her own driveway. She made her way to the back door and stumbled into the house. As she took off her wet coat and snow-covered boots, she heard a voice on the CB. It was her father!

". . . 21-21, Unit One to Base," the radio crackled. "You there, Pat?"

Pat ran over and picked up the mike. "This is me, Dad. I was over at Mrs. Lester's house." She told her father all about Mrs. Lester and her sick baby.

"Good work," Mr. Mitchell said. "I had trouble with the plow. I clipped a fire hydrant with a corner of the blade. One of the pins snapped off. I didn't have extra pins with me. Finally I had to use a wrench for a pin. I don't know how long it will hold."

"You could take a pin from the snowplow back here," Pat said.

"It would take too long to get back," Mr. Mitchell said. "I'm on my way to Doc Miller's house now. I don't like this rising wind. We may have some trees coming down."

"Or maybe a power blackout," Pat said.

"Yes, that could happen too. All right, I'll sign off now. Be in touch later."

"OK, Dad."

Pat put the mike down. She looked at the wall clock. Half past 12! Wow! She had not stayed up past midnight since last New Year's Eve.

Half an hour later the phone rang. "Hello?" answered Pat.

"This is Chief Campbell. Where is your dad, Pat? Russo managed to get Mrs. Lester and her baby over to Doc Miller's. But the doctor's driveway has to be plowed. I thought your father was on his way."

"I'll get him on the radio, Chief."

"You do that, Pat. Tell him to make it as quick as he can. We've got a very sick baby here."

"I'll call him right now," Pat said. She hung up the phone.

"KLI 21-21, Base to Unit One. Come in, Dad."

Pat waited and then tried again. No answer. She kept trying for a good five minutes. Finally she gave up and called the police.

"Chief? I can't get my dad on the radio."

The Chief sounded angry. "You can't get him! How about Wesley or Bill? Can you reach them?"

"No, sir. Only my dad's truck has a radio."

"Oh, have we got trouble! Doc says the Lester baby has viral pneumonia. We have to get him to an oxygen tent, but there are none on the island. We can't get to the mainland, either. The ferry has stopped running because of the storm. And I can't send the police launch. It would be suicide in this weather."

"How about the Coast Guard?" Pat asked.

"I've already called them. The only thing they will send is their cutter. And that has to come all the way from Boston. It won't be here until tomorrow noon. We might keep the baby alive if we got him to the firehouse. They have emergency oxygen bottles there. But Doc Miller's driveway is blocked. Russo only got halfway up the drive. Then he stalled."

"I'm sure my dad is on the way," Pat said. "He knows how serious it is."

"What if his truck broke down?" asked the Chief. "Where are Wesley and Bill with their trucks?"

"Bill is at French Cut," Pat said. "I don't know where Wesley is. My father knows."

"Now if we just knew where your dad was."

"How about a plane, Chief? Maybe someone could fly the baby to the mainland."

"In this storm? The pilot would have to be crazy. Anyway, the runways are bound to be blocked."

"I suppose you're right," Pat said slowly. "Still — "

"Look, Pat," the Chief interrupted. "If there were any way to get a plane out tonight, I'd be all for it. But I just don't think we have a chance. You'd better keep trying to reach your dad. I'll call back later."

37

"Yes, sir." Pat hung up the phone. Then she tried to call her dad on the radio. But she couldn't reach him. After 20 minutes of trying, Pat gave up. She went over to the back door to check on the snow. Just the tip of the ruler could be seen.

"Twelve inches already," Pat said out loud. "And it's still coming down." She went back to sit in front of the radio. If only there were some way she could help Mrs. Lester. If only she had called her in time. If only she hadn't forgotten that promise to her mother!

Then Pat had an idea. She thought of Leif Hope, the pilot who worked for Mr. Kerr. Arthur Kerr was a millionaire. He had a summer house on the island. He also had a private plane. Leif often flew Mr. Kerr back and forth between the island and the mainland. The plane was put away for the winter. Still, Leif might take the plane out if he knew that a baby's life was at stake. It was worth a call.

Pat looked up the number in the phone book. Then she called the Hope house, in Homeport. As she waited for someone to answer the phone, she noticed the time. It was almost two o'clock.

"Hello?"

"Mr. Hope?" Pat said. "This is Pat Mitchell. I'm sorry to call so late."

"You'd better be sorry. You woke me up. Are you Joe Mitchell's girl?"

38

"That's right, Mr. Hope. The thing is, there is an emergency. Can you fly someone to Boston?"

"In this weather? You must be crazy."

Pat told Leif Hope about Mrs. Lester's baby. As she talked, a plan formed in her mind. It just might work. "Mr. Hope, if the runway was clear of snow, could you take off?"

"I guess so. But who is going to clear the runway? And how do I get to the airport? And once I'm up in the air, how do I get down again? Where am I going to land in a storm like this?"

"Maybe the airport in Boston is clear," said Pat. "Or you could fly to Providence or Stamford. One of those airports has to be open."

"I wouldn't count on it," said Leif.

"But if an airport was open, you could do it?"

"I suppose so," Leif admitted. "But the runway here has to be plowed. And it has to be kept clean right up to the last minute."

Pat thought of the fourth snowplow that was out in the garage. Maybe she could find a way to use it despite the missing gas tank. "I think I can get a plow out to the runway," she told Leif.

"Fine. That's one problem solved. Now, how do you get me to the airport?" Leif asked.

"I'm working on that," Pat said.

"And how do you find me an open airport on the mainland?"

"I'm working on that too," Pat said.

"OK, you solve those problems. Then you call me back."

"How long will it take to get the plane ready?" Pat asked.

"Twenty minutes, maybe half an hour."

"All right, Mr. Hope. I'll call you back."

"You do that. Just fix up those little problems. Then call me." He said good-bye and hung up.

40

CHAPTER 6

Pat hung up the phone and sat staring at it. Leif had left her with some tough problems.

Once more she tried to reach her dad on the radio. But again she had no luck. She walked over to the back door and looked out. She couldn't see the ruler anymore. The snow was over 12 inches deep. She went back to the phone and dialed the O'Connors' number.

"Hello?" Mrs. O'Connor said.

"This is Pat, Mrs. O'Connor. I'm sorry to call you so late."

"That's all right, Pat. I wasn't sleeping anyway. I keep thinking of my husband out on his fishing boat. I hope he's not in the middle of all this."

"Maybe they outran the storm, Mrs. O'Connor."

"Let's hope so."

"Could I talk to Judy, please?"

"She's asleep. Can it wait until the morning?"

Pat told Mrs. O'Connor about the Lester baby. Then she told her about Leif Hope and the plane. "I was wondering, Mrs. O'Connor," she said. "Could Judy drive your snowmobile to Mr. Hope's house and then take him to the airport?"

"I'll wake her up and ask her," Mrs. O'Connor said. "But why can't your father come over? Couldn't he drive the snowmobile?"

Pat explained that her father was on the way to Doctor Miller's house. She told Mrs. O'Connor that French Cut was probably blocked. The airport, and their end of the island, was cut off.

"So you see, Mrs. O'Connor," Pat said, "the snowmobile is the only vehicle that can get Mr. Hope from the village to the airport."

"Yes, I can see that. Well, let me wake Judy."

"There's one more thing, Mrs. O'Connor."

"Yes?"

"I could use more help. Do you think Mrs. Dawson would let Vicky and Eddie come over?" The Dawsons lived right next door to the O'Connors.

"I think so. Do you want me to ask her?"

"Yes, please. And could Judy pick them up and bring them over here?"

"The snowmobile isn't supposed to carry more than two people," said Mrs. O'Connor. "A third

42

person could be dangerous."

"I know, but this is an emergency."

"All right, Pat. I'll see what I can do," Mrs. O'Connor promised.

Pat hung up the phone and went back to the radio. Once more she tried to contact her father, but there was still no answer.

Twenty minutes later Pat heard the buzz-saw sound of the snowmobile. Three kids jumped off and ran up to the back door. In a moment everyone was shouting questions.

"Hold it," Pat yelled. "OK, Judy, you take off and pick up Mr. Hope. Get him to the airport as soon as you can."

Judy got into the snowmobile and took off.

"All right," said Pat, "I want Vicky to help me on the snowplow. And I want Eddie to stay here and answer the radio and phone."

Pat showed Eddie how to operate the radio.

They tried to call her father again, but he still didn't answer. Pat told Eddie to keep trying to get her father. Then she and Vicky went out to the garage to work on the snowplow.

Pat lifted the hood of the truck. Then she climbed up on the fender. Looking down, she pointed. "This is the fuel pump," she told Vicky. "Somehow we have to get gas flowing through that line there, and then into this pump."

Pat hopped down from the fender and looked around the garage. Soon she spotted an empty five-gallon gas can. "We can use this," she said. A few minutes later she found an empty one-gallon can with a thin neck. Then she looked

around for some plastic tubing. When she didn't find it right away, she asked Vicky to keep searching. In the meantime, Pat took the two empty cans outside. She filled them with gas from a big 500-gallon drum. Then she went back into the garage.

"Is this what you were looking for?" asked Vicky, holding up a roll of white plastic tubing.

"That's it," said Pat. She unhooked the copper input line from the fuel pump. Then she fitted one end of the plastic tubing over the connection. It made a nice tight fit.

Next, Pat searched the inside of the cab. Finally she found a space beside the brake pedal. She pushed the tubing through the slot so it ran directly from the engine to the cab. Now all she had to do was connect the other end of the tubing to the five-gallon gas can.

That turned out to be a problem. The narrow tubing was too small to fit over the spout. But it did fit over the thinner spout of the one-gallon can. "We'll use the big can as an extra," Pat told Vicky. "When the small can is empty, we'll refill it from the larger can."

Then it was time to test the truck. Pat settled herself behind the steering wheel. Vicky sat beside her, holding the one-gallon gas can.

"Cross your fingers," Pat told Vicky. "If the truck doesn't work now, I don't know what else we can do."

CHAPTER 7

Pat turned the ignition key. The engine coughed once and then died. She waited a moment before she tried again.

"Do you know much about driving this truck?" asked Vicky.

"Oh, sure, I've turned it around in the yard."

"If you get this thing to the airport, you're a genius," Vicky said.

"I'll get us there. You hold the can steady. Make sure the piece of tubing doesn't slip off."

Once again Pat turned the key. Again the engine coughed briefly a couple of times. Pat pumped on the gas pedal. She wanted to give

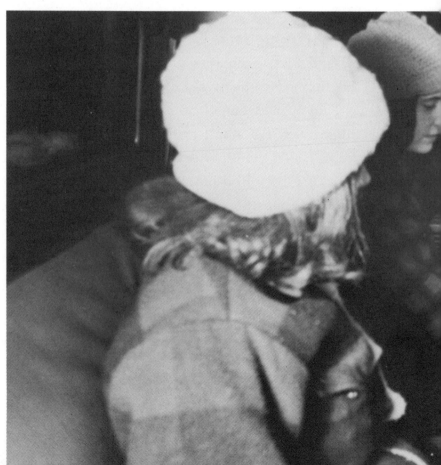

the carburetor another shot of gas. Suddenly one of the cylinders fired. More cylinders popped. Soon the engine was running smoothly.

"We did it!" Pat yelled.

"Hooray," shouted Vicky.

The motor sounded fine now. It ran with a nice, regular beat. Pat backed the truck out of the garage. In the yard she tested the hydraulic system. The snowplow blade jerked up. But Pat soon had the big blade moving smoothly up and down.

She shouted to Vicky. "Be back in a minute." Then she got out of the truck and ran into the kitchen. Eddie looked up from the radio.

"No luck with my dad?" Pat asked.

"Not yet."

"OK, keep trying," Pat told him. Then she went to the phone and dialed a number. "Mr. Hope? This is Pat Mitchell."

"Oh, yeah," Leif said. "The kid who believes in miracles, right?"

Pat shook her head. Adults, you couldn't tell them anything. "Mr. Hope, has the snowmobile reached you yet?"

"Snowmobile?"

Pat told him about Judy O'Connor. She also explained about the snowplow.

"Wait a minute," Leif said. "You mean you sent someone to pick me up? And you have a truck to plow off the runway?"

"That's right," said Pat.

"I can hardly believe it. All right, I'll get ready. We'll give it a try. In the meantime, you will get to the airport before me. Plow out a path from the big green hangar to the main runway. After that, keep plowing the main runway."

"OK, Mr. Hope."

"We still have one problem," Leif pointed out. "I don't know what the weather is like on the mainland."

"Can you call the Chief of Police?" Pat asked. "Maybe he can reach someone on the radio-telephone hookup."

"Hey, that's a great idea," Leif said. "In fact, the Chief can contact Boston Airport. They'll find me a field open somewhere on the mainland. All right, Pat, you get going. I'll call the Chief and meet you at the airport."

Pat hung up with a grin. Maybe she had talked an adult into believing in miracles too.

"OK," she called to Eddie. "We're off to the airport."

"Good luck!" said Eddie.

Pat went back outside and climbed up into the truck. Then she grinned at Vicky. The motor was running nice and smoothly.

"Hold on, I'm going to drop the blade," Pat yelled above the noise of the engine. In a moment the blade was down. It threw a wave of white snow out in front of the truck. Pat stopped at the bottom of the driveway. She decided to raise the blade. They would go faster if they

didn't have to plow. It was only three miles to the airport. But every minute counted.

For a while they moved ahead at a good speed. Then the truck hit a snow drift. Pat had to drop the blade. Back and forth went the plow. The snow built up along the side of the road. Then the drift was cut open.

Once more Pat raised the blade. The truck moved ahead. But soon they hit another drift. Pat backed up and dropped the blade. Then she turned to Vicky. "How is the gas holding out?"

Vicky lifted the can. She shook it gently back and forth. "About half full, I think."

"Good. That should get us to the airport."

They cut through the drift. Then they hit another one. It was slow going, but finally they reached the airport road. Pat dropped the blade and cleared a path to the large green hangar. Then she headed for the main runway. When she got there, Pat switched off the engine. "Time to refuel," she told Vicky.

Vicky lifted the gallon can. "Yes," she said. "It feels almost empty." She slipped the plastic tubing off the spout. Then she unscrewed the cap of the large can. "We should pour this outside. Without a funnel, we're going to spill some."

"You're right," Pat agreed. She and Vicky climbed out of the truck. Pat held the smaller can while Vicky filled it with gas from the larger one. Then they got back into the truck. Vicky put the plastic tubing back on the small can. Then she placed the can between her knees.

A minute later, they saw a bright light moving through the trees. "That must be Judy and Mr. Hope in the snowmobile," said Pat.

"Yes," said Vicky. "They're headed for the hangar."

Just then they saw someone jump off the snowmobile. The small red machine made a wide turn and raced off. "Now where is she going?" Vicky asked.

"I don't know," said Pat. "But we are going to find out."

CHAPTER 8

Pat and Vicky drove over to the hangar. Leif was there, waiting. "Hi, girls," he called.

"Hi, Mr. Hope," said Pat. "Where did Judy go?"

"Back for Doc Miller and the baby."

"How long will it take her?"

"Oh, maybe half an hour," Leif said.

"Will you be ready by then?" asked Pat.

"I hope so. Will the runway be ready for me?"

Pat took the hint. She and Vicky got into the truck and headed back to the runway.

Pat and Vicky made half a dozen passes down the runway. They cleared away most of the snow. Then they went back to the hangar. "Is the runway clear?" Leif asked the girls.

"Yes," said Pat and Vicky at the same time.

"Good," said Leif. "Now all we have to do is call the Chief at the police station. He should have been able to reach Boston Airport by now. If they have found a place for me to land, then

I'll take off. But if they haven't . . ." Leif glanced at Pat's worried face. Then he pointed to a large building. "The phone is in the operations building over there."

"We can drive over in the truck," said Pat.

A short while later, they pulled up in front of the operations building. Leif led the way to the office. He picked up the phone and dialed the police station. Then he shook his head and hung up. "I was afraid of that," he said. "In a storm like this, the lines are always busy."

Leif tried to make the call a few more times. But each time, he had to hang up. Finally, he sat down beside Pat and Vicky. "We'll wait a little while," he said. "Then we'll try again." He yawned and closed his eyes.

Pat looked over at Vicky. Her friend's eyes were closing too. How could anyone sleep at a time like this? Pat wondered.

Pat got up and walked over to the window. The snow was still coming down. She thought of trying the police station again. But just then she saw a flash of red off in the distance. It was the snowmobile!

"They made it," Pat shouted. "Come and see." Her cries woke Vicky and Leif. They got up and joined Pat at the window. When the snowmobile reached the operations building, Judy and Doc Miller got out. The doctor had Mrs. Lester's baby in his arms.

CHAPTER 9

"How is the baby?" Pat asked Doctor Miller as they entered the office.

"Not well, I'm afraid," replied the doctor. "But I think he'll pull through, if we can get him to the hospital."

"Can the plane take off?" Judy asked.

"Yes," said Pat. "But Leif has to have clearance first."

At the sound of his name, Leif looked up from the phone. He covered the mouthpiece with his hand. "It's ringing," he said. Suddenly his face brightened. "Hello, Chief?"

Pat's heart gave a leap. Leif had finally gotten through!

"What? I can't hear you!" Leif shouted. "OK, got it. Boston? Ceiling one thousand? Visibility two miles? Fine. I'll take off, then. Yes. These crazy kids have done it. Yes. See you."

Leif put down the phone. Then he was all action. "Let's get this show on the road."

Doctor Miller stood up from his chair. He held the baby in his arms. "How long will it take to reach Boston?" he asked.

"Less than an hour," Leif said. "Pat, it's still snowing, so you'll have to clear the runway again. I'm going to get into the plane now, with Doc Miller and the baby. I want you to be plowing right ahead of me. I'll follow you down the runway. That way I can be sure it will be clear all the way."

"We're on our way," Pat said. She turned to Vicky and Judy. "Come on," she said, "let's get going."

The girls hurried outside to the truck. Vicky sat beside Pat, holding the can of gas. Judy held the tubing over the spout.

They drove to the end of the runway. Pat plowed a head start for 20 yards or so. Then she waited for the plane to catch up.

The red and white wing lights came closer. The plane turned onto the runway behind them. Leif warmed up the motor for a good five minutes.

Pat kept looking in the rearview mirror. She heard the plane's motor rev up. Then she saw Leif lift his arm. He waved the truck on ahead.

Pat turned her lights on and off. Then she smiled across at Vicky and Judy. "Hang on, here we go!" Quickly Pat shifted into second gear. Then she started plowing the snow. From time to time she looked in the mirror. She saw that the plane had already started its run.

Pat pushed down on the gas pedal and shifted into third. They were doing 30 now. The snow was moving out in a big wave in front of the plow. Suddenly the truck's motor coughed. Pat yelled in a panicky voice, "How's our . . .?"

Vicky shook the can and cried, "I think we're out of gas!"

The motor was still running on the gas that was in the tube. But that would not last long, Pat knew.

"Quick! Vicky, yank off the tubing," said Pat. "Judy, see if you can pour in some gas from the big can."

Judy began to pour from the five-gallon can. Vicky tried to hold the small can steady, but gas splashed all over the seat. Finally, Vicky and Judy managed to fill up the smaller can.

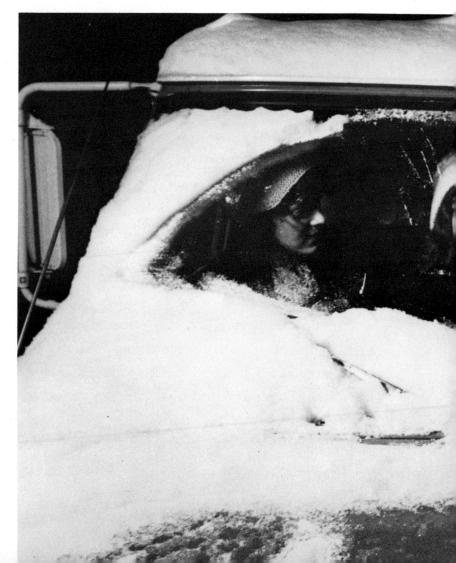

Just when Pat thought they were safe, the motor died. Pat tried to restart the engine, but it wouldn't catch. The truck was still moving, but slowly. And the plane was less than 50 yards behind them now.

Pat looked in the rearview mirror. The plane was still moving toward them. She could see Leif's face. It was grim. He'd never be able to stop the plane in time to keep it from crashing into the truck. Pat knew she had to do

something — and fast.

Maybe she could turn off into the snowbank at the side of the runway. But would there be enough room for the plane to get by? Probably not, Pat decided. At best, it would be a tight squeeze and very risky. Too risky, Pat realized.

There was only one other thing Pat could do. She could try to start the truck by putting it into second gear and quickly letting out the clutch. Then she would have to pray that the engine would start. If it did start, she could plow the rest of the runway ahead of the plane. But if the engine didn't start, the plane would run right into the back of the truck. With all the gas that had been spilled, there would surely be a fire.

None of them would survive. Pat was sure of it.

She took one more look at the plane. Then she made up her mind. She would try to get down the runway, no matter what. She shifted into second gear and let the clutch jerk out. The truck began to buck. It bucked half a dozen times. Pat pushed in the clutch again. Then she let it bounce out once more. She looked in the mirror. The plane was too close behind them. Even if she managed to get the truck started, it might be too late.

"Pray!" screamed Pat. She would try it one more time. If it didn't start, she would tell the others to jump. Then she would open her door and hope there was time for her to jump, too.

CHAPTER 10

The truck bucked once more. Then the engine caught in a quick series of explosions. Pat eased out the choke. If she stalled now, it was all over. She felt the engine settle down.

By now the plane was within a few yards of the truck. Pat rammed the gear shift into high. She prayed that the truck would take the sudden pull. She had to build up more speed.

There was a second's hesitation. Then the truck leaped forward. "We're too late!" Vicky cried out. "The plane is on top of us."

"Duck!" Judy screamed.

Pat looked in the mirror. All she could see was the underside of the plane. A sudden roar filled the truck.

Pat threw up her hands. She was sure they were going to crash. But the roar died down. Pat looked up. Right there, in front of the windshield, was the tail end of the plane. Its wing lights were blinking on and off. The plane climbed away, and Pat knew it was going to make it.

The truck bumped to a stop in a three-foot wall of snow. Pat folded her arms. Then she said a prayer of thanks.

Vicky and Judy were both talking at the same time. Pat couldn't make out what they were saying. Her hands were trembling, but she managed to turn the truck around.

Judy leaned over and clapped Pat on the

back. "You were terrific, Pat. No kidding."

"You scared me to death," Vicky said.

For a while they talked about their narrow escape. But it had been a long night, and the girls decided it was time to go home.

"Judy, you drive the snowmobile to my house and pick up Eddie," said Pat. "Then take him home. After that, come back for Vicky."

"Why can't I take Vicky now?" Judy asked.

"Because Pat needs me to help drive the truck," said Vicky.

"That's right," Pat said. She and Vicky grinned at each other.

Half an hour later everyone had gone home. Pat put the truck away in the garage. She thought about everything that had happened. "Wait until Dad hears about this," Pat thought. "He'll never call me irresponsible again."

Pat was closing the garage door when she saw something leaning against the wall. It was her 10-speed bike. She went over and took a close look. The bike had a flat tire, and it needed a good oiling. Half an hour with some steel wool would take care of those rust spots on the frame. Pat promised herself that she'd work on the bike tomorrow. She would prove to her dad that she could look after her things. Then maybe he'd let her get that trail bike.

Pat left the garage and walked to the house. The snow had stopped. Here and there a star was beginning to show through.

In the kitchen, the radio crackled to life. Pat sat down and picked up the mike. "KLI 21-21, Base to Unit One. Come in, Dad."

"Unit One to Base. This is Joe Mitchell. You there, Pat?"

"Got you, Dad."

Mr. Mitchell explained that a ball of frozen slush had pulled loose a radio wire. He had been without the radio for over two hours. He was now with Mrs. Lester at Doctor Miller's house. "How have things been with you, Pat?"

"No problems, Dad. Everything is fine. Tell Mrs. Lester that her baby is going to be OK."

"She knows. The Chief just called her. We're going to tackle French Cut now. We should have it open in an hour or so. Can you stay on the radio until I get home?"

"Sure, Dad."

"By the way, how could that plane take off with the runway not plowed?"

"It's a long story, Dad. I'll tell you all about it when you get home."

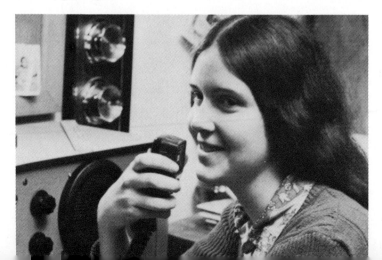